Lil' Magdalene

Steven Charles Ross

Order Online
451Publishing.com

lilmagdalene.com

451 Publishing

He got tired of holding the scrap of paper up
in the wind.

He pressed the brakes and slowed the car.

He hated that he wouldn't let go.

Flapping in the wind.

A torn little flag flapping in the wind.

He tucked it into his shirt pocket and put
both hands back on the steering wheel.

Never take it out of your wallet.

His mother had ripped up some sheets of paper,

tossing them into his father's grave.

The wind blew one piece up and

against his shoe.

He picked it up.

His mom's handwriting.

In crayon.

Embarrassed.

He slid it into his pants pocket.

Later, he read it.

Even now, years later, he couldn't let go of it.

A scrap of paper.

Crayon colors.

He drove up to an empty crossroad

in the middle of nowhere and

turned the radio static off.

Last night he had slept in his car on some lost

dirt road.

For breakfast he was chewing on a somewhat

stale tuna salad sandwich and drinking

his last can of Coca-Cola.

He was reviewing those last couple of
hours before he had left town.

He usually enjoyed debriefings.

They were like a pat on the back by
respectful colleagues.

That psychologist however, was just crap.

A female on a debriefing team.

How did he feel?

How did he really feel?

It was obscene – she's an idiot.

He bit his tongue, but a snort escaped, so they all started laughing . . . but not her.

And debriefings were supposed to be serious, so he tapped his folders and went cool.

He was a professional.

"Gentlemen, shall we wrap this up?"

Always cool . . . tap, tap.

This was of no concern.

Didn't matter much.

Nope.

But . . .

FUCK THEM.

Anyway, that was days ago.

He spat over the window.

Wiped his nose with his sleeve.

No meetings.

No mission.

No agenda.

Beer and sandwiches in the cooler.

No more thinking.

It was, "adios amigos."

He wiggled cautiously and massaged his
neck, sore from the night's sleep.

He thought he saw some wildflowers blooming
on the side of the road to the left.

His eyes squinted and he smiled somewhat.

His engine was rumbling.

He turned left and drove faster and faster.

He loved to drive his beautiful car.

The open road.

Any road.

It was springtime.

He felt calm.

For long periods of time, he had been forgetting to turn the radio on.

Just whistling.

Whistling and driving.

He recalled, late last night, somewhere,

he had crossed the Mississippi.

He didn't know where, Green something,

because out here, he tried to ignore

those kinds of signs.

He remembered thinking . . . one more river.

He was from the East Coast, the Old Dominion,
but well out, Appalachia.

A small Anglo type community, mostly Scottish
with the usual Protestant blend additives.

He hadn't been back to his hometown for
about two years.

Not since they buried his father at Arlington.

His father was with those Virginia boys, when
they got slaughtered on a beach they named
"Bloody Omaha."

That story was never spoken of.

When his father was able to write letters

home again, he was somehow an officer.

Patton's Third Army.

Racing across France.

He survived the war on account of his foot

being sawed off near the town of Bastogne.

So, he was lucky to have been born many years later.

An only child raised to be a true American by devoted Christian parents.

His father would tell him about that war.

Soldier brothers taking turns saving each other . . . sharing food and heartbreak . . . killing the bad guys . . . killing for America!

"CHICKAMAUGA - PA"

"Shush-boy"

Shhhhhhhhhhhhhhh

They made the best possible bed time stories.

Many more years later his father would tell

him that he would fight the cancer long

enough to see a grandson.

Then further along . . . the episodes.

Day after day . . . week after week.

The shakes.

The murmurs.

The screams.

His clean-cut, soft-spoken father,

trapped in a cancer-induced,

time-warped nightmare.

Landing on Omaha Beach.

Over and over and over.

Sweet Jesus.

And in the lucid moments,

no little grandson to comfort

those weary bugged-out eyes.

The car drifted along

and so did he.

He found himself musing those tender days . . .

playing catch with his hero . . .

his magic footed father.

But those memories were ruined.

Pierced by his dying screams.

"Kill them!"

"Kill them!"

"Kill them goddam snipers!"

He drove with an empty head for some

period of time.

Then on a long straightaway, his mind

spun and slid through countless

dozens of women.

A few years back, he'd had a sorority-type.

She was his all-time favorite piece of pie.

The affair lasted a couple of months.

He reckoned it mostly his fault.

She would cry about secrets and lying.

And he hated ballet, opera, theatre.

All that crap.

When he first met her.

A beach house.

Endless guest bedrooms.

The usual company weekend party.

She was tiptoeing around.

Dressed like, "I Dream of Jeannie."

Tray of snacks and a fancy tequila bottle.

They walked away together and found

a bed beyond the crowd.

Soon they were talking like old friends.

He, she . . . and the blue agave.

Eventually, they spoke of anthropology.

Her field of expertise, doctorate program.

Her thesis paper, research, was that males were naturally-selected sexual predators.

He needed time on that one, he said.

Later on, he was pointing out the natural proclivity of the young female to stray too far from Daddy's cave.

Teasing statements.

Dilated pupils.

Nipples.

Yep.

He took a large bite of the tuna sandwich.

He chewed on the possibility . . . maybe

that night wasn't really a very good way

to start a long-term relationship anyway.

What?

That's crap.

Shut up.

Just shut up.

He fumbled around in the cooler next to him and found a Budweiser.

He popped it open, took a long draw and tucked the icy can in his crotch.

He gripped the steering wheel tight and floored the gas pedal.

He started whistling.

Whistling and driving.

Back in his home town, a superstore had

replaced most of the town's shops.

The butcher.

The baker.

He remembered them all.

His cousins even had to close the family

hardware store.

His mom had told him that everyone locked

their doors now, even when they were home.

This all disgusted him . . .

so he didn't think about it.

He just didn't think about them anymore.

Somehow he'd lost track of when he last talked with his mom over the phone. Seemingly meaningless conversations, friends, family, remains of a farm, and finally, inevitably . . . "son, you're a good boy."

He took a deep breath and relaxed his grip on the steering wheel.

He turned the radio on and searched for a station.

Again, there was nothing but static and church music.

He turned it off.

Church music was crap.

It was a long drive from his office to reach

these wide open spaces.

He didn't care.

Out here it seemed like he had plenty of time.

He believed that this balanced him with time.

Like when time really ticked.

When time really ticked with life and death.

Some of the guys used to kid him about these road trips.

Why didn't he go to exotic places anymore?

Hell, the government paid for it.

They were given anything they needed.

Or wanted.

European sports cars.

Expensive booze.

Bungalows on any beach.

First-class whores.

Caymen bank accounts.

Plenty of cash.

"Hey, don't we earn this?"

Sure thing.

But the last couple of years, for the

most part, he just didn't care.

He liked to drive around the country.

Our country.

Driving his car.

That's what made him feel right.

During these times away, he never bothered

with getting drunk.

Heavy drinking really wasn't

professional behavior.

His hand reached over and into the cooler.

He was very much a professional.

Educated.

Athletic.

A straight-talking kind of guy.

He was starting to become a legend in the isolated community of top secret government service.

His attitude was excellent.

A – okay.

All the way.

He just loved to spend about a week driving around and visiting small hometown communities.

Sleeping peacefully in quaint out-of-the-way places and learning the history of the area from some old timer.

And, he loved this car.

This car . . . was built with power.

This car, was an Infantry blue, 1960, Chevrolet

Impala convertible.

V-8, Turbo Thrust, Turbo Glide . . . yes.

Seats, reupholstered, white leather.

She had lots of chrome and shined like new.

The day he was born, his father paid

for her in cash.

Special order . . . delivered from Texas.

The money, was from some kind of

bank account back in England.

His dad only used her for church, occasional

Sunday drives and rare family road trips with

awkward whispers with mother.

And now it was his.

He kept her tiptop and ready to road trip.

He always drove when he could,

with her top down.

This made him feel closer to America.

Especially this America . . . way out here.

Sometimes while he was driving he would
review his career.

He thought he had not volunteered too often.

He likened his career to dominoes.

One move seemed to click into another.

Yet always bringing something else
along with it.

It was 1988, and time was moving faster.

He had a growing secret envy of other men
with wives and children, living what must be
wonderful lives out here in the heartland.

Fixing things.

Creating stuff.

America.

As he drove and drove, it didn't matter

to him where he was.

He couldn't get lost.

He was already where he wanted to be, and

wherever he was headed was fine with him.

Just being out here.

Out here . . . the air he needed to breathe.

America.

Too many times in his life, he had to know

exactly where he was, down to the precise

step at the precise time.

But out here, he didn't have to look at

signs if he didn't want to.

And he did not want to.

Not out here.

Into the morning hours he drove through

forest and farm country.

He began traveling up and down hills.

He had stopped only once to stretch, pee, and

take his convertible top down.

The cool air felt wet and sweet rushing by

as he flew upon the outskirts of another

small apple-pie town.

There was such an abundance of wildflowers

on both sides of the road that

the effect was dizzying.

He caught himself daydreaming about that "I Dream of Jeannie" chick.

He adjusted his trousers, touched the brakes, slid off the road a bit, and over-adjusted across the center line.

He didn't catch the town's welcome sign.

The center of the little town had a large plain white church with a tall steeple and a park with a picnic area.

A riot of wildflowers.

It was all very picturesque.

It looked like all of the people in the surrounding area were gathered in front of the church, preparing to go inside.

Probably, today was a Sunday.

Cars were parked everywhere.

He drove around the town square twice and pulled into the last open space.

The car bounced over the curb and into their park.

He decided to turn the motor off and sit awhile.

He lifted up his sunglasses and looked

them over with keen blue eyes.

All dressed up, happy Christian folks,

who just knew they were all

going to heaven.

Then it hit . . . they might not want him

in their nice heaven.

A good boy?

They might hate him.

They would put him on the express

elevator to hell.

Right then, he felt like he was already on it.

Had been for years.

Although he tried not to, he thought about his friend and mentor, Major ███████████

He had recently died . . . shot in the gut.

An isolated airfield in Panama.

[bankrabbits] ? [fubar] ?

What mistake did he make?

Was it a fluke shot?

Professional?

They just didn't know.

Not yet.

His right hand took the scrap of paper

out of his shirt pocket.

He twisted and folded, then flicked it up

into their faces.

His right trigger finger

started twitching

spastically.

His anger grew with a terrible pain.

His belly, as if he too, were gut-shot.

Quickly it grew into hatred with a crashing
mental and physical nausea.

He swallowed roughly and yelled,

"Bastards."

He jerked on the door handle and staggered
out of the car, growling.

He fell to his knees, then hands, as vomit
started gushing out of his nose
and mouth.

He was puking and screaming, and the violence

eclipsed with dry heaving agony and

incoherent blasphemy.

He wished for death.

The elevator snapped and he began falling.

Screaming into madness.

Screaming

heaving

screaming

heaving

screaming . . .

With tunnel-like vision, he observed a
very small female child in a white dress
walking towards him.

She held a bouquet of flowers in her hands.

All the members of the congregation stood
frozen on the church steps and under
the trees.

When she was across the street and into the
park, he heard a female voice echoing.

"Katie . . . come . . . back!"

But she would not.

It was like she created a bizarre psycho bungee cord, holding him, pulling him towards her by his intestines.

Closing his throat.

He wanted her to go away, but he became

soundless . . . frozen.

With each step she took, the intense hatred

faded into a mind-wrenching buzzing.

He completely fixated on the girl and the

flowers, growing ever larger through

the tunnel.

When she was about fifty paces away . . .

his ears popped.

It started happening.

Like a slide projection wheel out of control.

His brain reviewed his whole career.

Flash.

Infantry basic training.

Flash.

Airborne.

Flash.

Special Forces.

Flash.

Pathfinder.

Flash.

Sniper school.

Flash . . . Flash . . . Flash . . .

His recruitment into government service.

Every mission, one by one.

Flash . . . Flash . . . Flash . . .

It was happening so quickly.

But he accepted it.

Calm and numb.

Staring between the flashes.

The little girl.

The flowers.

Coming ever closer through the tunnel.

When he finally flashed to it, he kept

flashing on his most recent mission.

He used to love his work.

The Cold War had a heroic quality about it.

He would die if he had to, exterminating all

the Marxist enslavers.

But now, his job was different.

Just so different.

These so called "drug lord" types, sometimes

hedged on their usual security, when having

a pleasant afternoon with their families.

Then all hell breaks loose.

Right out of the blue sky.

Flash.

The look of shock and disbelief on the wife's face, with husband's bloody brains cradled in her lap.

He had shot high.

Flash.

Two little boy twins, jumping around, freaked, like they were being yanked by some crazed puppeteer.

Flash.

The wife?

Creative accountant – Secondary Target.

Mother . . .

Flash.

Shot her.

Flash.

Shot her.

Flash.

Shot . . . oh-shit.

Flash.

Only one little boy, kneeling . . . now

a pocket knife up in the . . .

waiting . . .

Pow.

Flash.

The picture show came to an abrupt end,

when the little girl stopped beside him.

Without a word, she held out the bouquet

of flowers, like the wildflowers that

were everywhere.

His stone-cold hands grasped the flowers.

Felt her warm, vibrating little fingers.

He saw the look on her little face.

Love in her eyes, deep into his.

He tried to smile.

She smiled, turned and then started skipping.

Back to her family, her people.

They were still frozen in time.

He was staring as if the world had stopped.

As if time had stopped ticking.

Only the little girl was in motion.

The spell was broken when she reached
the arms of her father and was pulled up
and around into the air.

Everything started moving again.

Where on earth was he?

Staring in a daze, on his knees, holding a
bouquet of wildflowers, somewhere in the
heartland of America.

He knew he'd just had some kind of

traumatic experience.

He breathed deeply and felt like . . .

he didn't know . . .

He felt good and wondered if he could

describe it or somehow write this down.

The back of his neck . . . what was that?

Somehow, his body was physically filled.

He felt connected to all creation.

Wonderfully alive on the miracle planet.

He was a giant to the microscopic, and then a tiny spark on a magic ball, circling a star in an infinite universe.

He felt free.

In the land of the free.

He thought of that little girl and whispered.

"And the home of the brave."

With wobbly knees, he got back into his car.

But he didn't feel like leaving.

And where would he go now?

He looked across the street at the courthouse.

This flag in the morning breeze.

He saw those red stripes.

Little stars in blue.

It felt different.

It felt alive.

It wasn't owned by a government.

This flag . . . was born in revolution.

Stitched for each and every patriot.

We the people . . .

He sat there for a while.

Just staring.

Eventually, he reached for a paper towel.

He wiped off his face and then gargled with beer.

He put an ice cube into his mouth.

Leaned his head back, shut his eyes,

and completely relaxed.

When I awoke, my forehead was pressed

against the steering wheel.

I saw the bloody red stain down my

white shirt.

I stared at the incredibly colorful, beautiful

flowers on my lap.

Think.

My shoulder exploded?

Think.

I rolled my head off the steering wheel and

fell across the floorboard . . . another bullet

smashed through the windshield.

Holy shit!

How possible?

Think.

How?

Cocaine.

Think.

Tracking device . . .

on my car.

Where was I?

What to do?

How no gun?

Idiot!

I decided I should . . . would . . . get to
the church.

I grabbed the flowers and slid carefully
out of the car.

My left arm didn't function.

I started walking.

I pressed the bouquet firmly against the

bleeding bullet hole as I walked over

a sea of wildflowers.

I heard a silenced bullet fly

past my head.

Bad shot.

Then another . . . bad shot.

Two shooters.

There were bullets crackling in

the tree branches.

Pathetic.

I fell on the church steps and heard a bullet

whack against the church above me.

Good shot.

I crawled up the steps, pulled myself

together and casually opened the door.

I started looking for a place to sit.

The church was packed full.

Many people were standing.

As my steps brought me further down the

aisle, more and more heads turned.

The preacher stopped the sermon and

gestured for me to come to him.

My legs stopped and my arm fell.

I dropped the flowers.

.

Then that little girl took hold of my

bloody hand.

Again, I felt her strange, yet not so strange,

powerful energy.

With every step, I found myself feeling better,

until it seemed like I was walking on air.

Time . . . ticked with my heartbeat.

The elderly preacher had a kind, strong face.

It felt like somehow, we recognized

each other.

I heard some argument about water.

Water was splashed on my head.

I remember him wiping my face with

his shirt sleeve . . .

Clear! . . . Bang!

It was a heck of a scene when I opened my

eyes in the emergency room.

The blur of hands and noise . . . clamps . . .

suction . . . Federal Agent . . . O-positive.

Blood . . . tubes . . . needles . . . naked.

I drifted around and watched for a while.

Then I passed out again.

How strange was that spring day.

It was a Sunday all right.

Easter Sunday.

Later that evening . . . I awoke.

Somebody or something spoke.

Surely I was heavily sedated.

Dreaming wildly.

About flowers.

I found all manifestations of flowers.

Flowers to keep.

Flowers to cast away.

Flowers that stay silent.

Flowers that must speak.

Hallucinating and yet, understanding things
that I could never clearly tell.

Especially about those . . . the flowers

of the heart-land.

It was from here . . . I heard.

Hey there you . . . happy birth-day.